NORWEGIAN SEA

NORTH
SEA

NORWAY

SWEDEN

Skagerrak

Kattegat

DENMARK

Gulf of Bothnia

FINLAND

Gulf of Finland

BALTIC SEA

GERMANY

GODS AND GODDESSES
OF THE
ANCIENT NORSE

GODS AND GODDESSES

OF THE

ANCIENT NORSE

Leonard
Everett
Fisher

Holiday House   New York

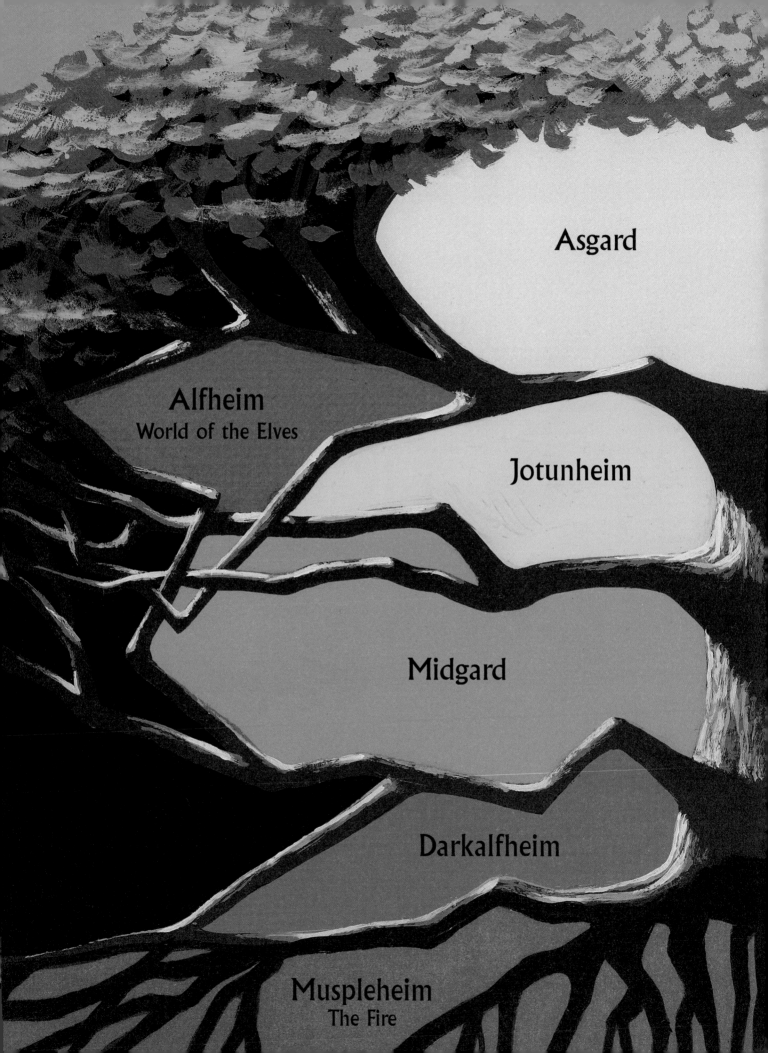

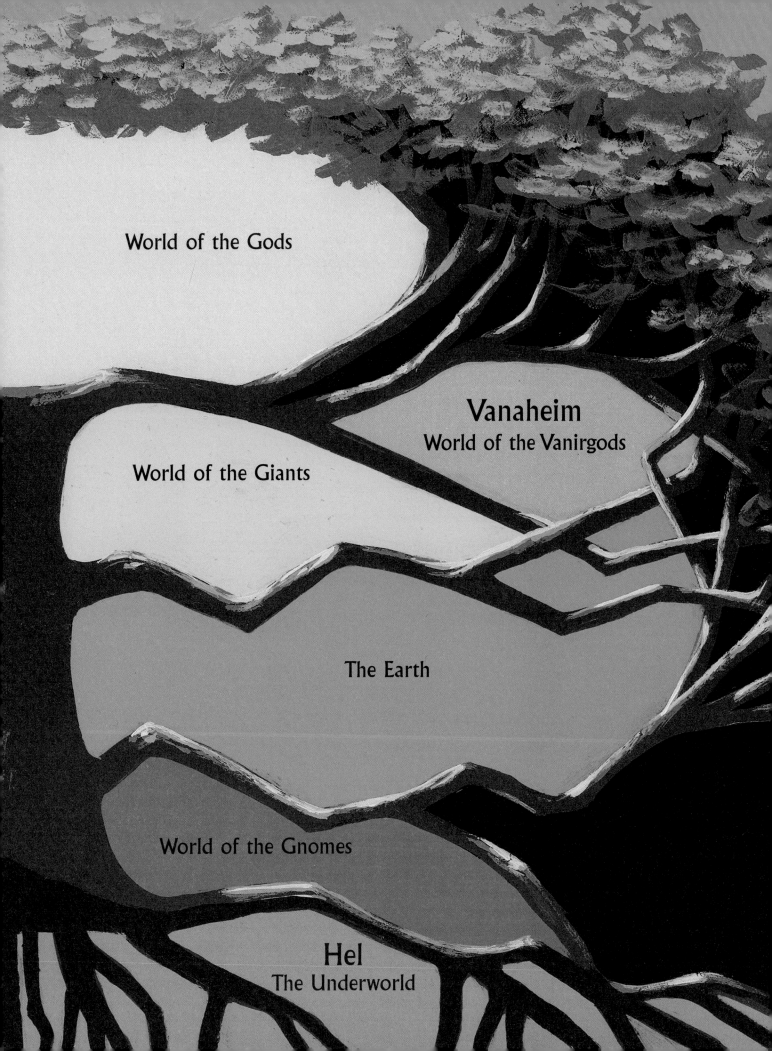

To Regina Griffin,
L. E. F.

Library of Congress Cataloging-in-Publication Data

Fisher, Leonard Everett.
Gods and goddesses of the ancient Norse / Leonard Everett Fisher.—1st ed.
p. cm.
Includes bibliographical references.
ISBN 0-8234-1569-4 (hardcover)
1. Gods, Norse—Juvenile literature. 2. Goddesses, Norse—Juvenile literature.
3. Mythology, Norse—Juvenile literature. [1. Mythology, Norse.] I. Title.
BL860 .F53 2001
293'.211—dc21   00-032040

INTRODUCTION

The ancient Norse believed that their gods and goddesses, the Aesir, lived above the clouds in Asgard, in gold and silver palaces. Humans lived below on Earth, which the Norse called Midgard. The Aesir could travel back and forth between Asgard and Earth by a rainbow bridge. But humans could not walk upon the rainbow bridge, and so could not reach the heavens.

A Norse warrior who fought for a good cause and died in battle could enter Asgard. Odin, the King of the Aesir, promised these men glorious afterlives in Valhalla, his great Hall of the Dead. His warrior-maidens, the Valkyries, joined by Freya, the Goddess of Love, gathered up the dead from each battlefield and carried them in triumph to Valhalla.

But, according to the Norse, nothing would last forever—not humans, not the warriors of Valhalla, not even the Aesir. Sometime in the future, a final battle would rage between the gods and evil. In this battle, which was called Ragnarok, the Aesir would fight their enemies, the hideous giants of Jotunheim, and all would perish. Nothing would be left.

To the ancient Norse, Ragnarok would be a victory, not a defeat. By their heroic death, the Aesir would prevent evil from overcoming the Earth.

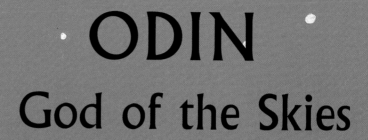

ODIN
God of the Skies

Odin, or Woden, the supreme ruler
of the Norse gods, lived alone in
Gladsheim, a glittering palace in Asgard.
Odin ate next to nothing. Instead, he gave his food to two wolves,
Geri and Freki, who sat at his feet. Two ravens, Hugin and Munin—
Thought and Memory—perched on his shoulders. Every day the two
birds would fly over the universe and return with news for Odin.

Odin craved wisdom. But to attain it, he
had to suffer. He gave up an eye in order to
drink from a magical well of knowledge.
He allowed his body to be hurt to learn
the mysterious writings called "runes." At
the risk of losing his powers, he stole a special
drink from a giantess that made anyone who drank it a poet. But Odin
accepted these costs gladly, because they brought him wisdom and
poetry, which he then gave to humans.

The fourth day of the week,
Wednesday, is named for Odin.

FRIGGA
Goddess of Marriage

Frigga was Odin's favorite wife. She spent much of her time spinning gold into thread at her palace, Fensalir. But no one in Asgard, not even Odin, knew what the thread was for—only Frigga. The ancient Norse believed Frigga knew many secrets of heaven and earth, but Frigga never shared what she knew with anyone.

Frigga was the goddess of family love and the home. Her most important role was as a kind and loving wife and mother. With Odin she had a son, Baldur, the God of Peace and Light, who was much loved by the Aesir.

Many of the ancient Norse believed that the sixth day of the week, Friday, was named for Frigga.

THOR
God of Thunder

Fiery, redheaded Thor was the oldest of Odin's many sons. He roamed the heavens in a goat-drawn chariot, chasing, challenging, and destroying evil giants and demons.

Thor possessed three remarkable gifts: iron gloves, a great hammer, and a magical belt that doubled his already enormous strength.

The rumble of his chariot made thunder, the strikes of his hammer lightning. Sparks flew from the wheels of his chariot as he charged through the sky.

Thor and his hammer were inseparable. Whenever he threw it across the sky, striking giants and demons with deadly fury, the hammer would return to him.

Despite his fierceness, Thor was a kind and generous god. He loved great feasts and was devoted to his wife, the gold-haired Sifi, and their two sons, Magni and Modi.

Thursday, the fifth day of the week, is named for him.

BALDUR
God of Peace and Light

Handsome Baldur, the only son of Frigga and Odin, was the most loved god in Asgard. But Baldur was destined to have a short life, and his death would be the first tragedy among the Aesir.

Baldur dreamed he was in danger, but he had no idea what the danger might be. His adoring mother traveled throughout the universe asking every living thing for a promise not to hurt him. She only skipped one small, seemingly harmless plant: the mistletoe. Odin himself asked Hela, the Goddess of Death, to refuse to receive Baldur.

To demonstrate Frigga's success, a game was held. The Aesir hurled stones, arrows, spears, swords, knives, even axes at Baldur. Nothing injured him. But cunning Loki, who was always out for trouble, figured out a way to kill him.

Loki knew that Frigga had missed the mistletoe plant. So he coaxed Baldur's blind half brother, Holdur, into throwing a twig of mistletoe at Baldur. The mistletoe struck Baldur in the heart, instantly killing him. All of the Aesir mourned Baldur, none more so than Nanna, his wife, who died of grief.

HERMOD
God of Courage

Hermod was a warrior god. As one of Odin's sons, he was Baldur's half brother. After Baldur's death, he volunteered to ride to Hel, the underworld, and offer a ransom for his brother's return. Odin loaned him his coal black, eight-legged horse, Steipmur, and Hermod galloped off to Hel.

Nine days and nine nights later, Hermod reached the bridge over the icy stream that separated the land of the living from Hel. He offered Hela, the Goddess of Death, anything she wanted in exchange for Baldur's return. But Hela told Hermod that she would only release Baldur if every single living thing shed a tear for him.

When Hermod returned, he told Frigga what Hela had offered. Frigga begged every living creature to cry for Baldur. All living things agreed, all except one old hag giant. She refused, saying she had never liked Baldur. Upon hearing that news, Hela refused to release Baldur.

The old hag giant was never seen again. But the Aesir realized that the old hag was Loki himself. And they vowed to take their revenge.

LOKI
"God" of Mischief

Loki was not a member of the Aesir—he was one of the giants, the Aesir's enemies. And yet he was as handsome as the Aesir, not ugly or misshapen like the other giants. But his good looks and playful presence hid a spiteful and wicked nature.

Because Odin had sworn brotherhood to him, Loki lived among the Aesir, even though he caused them endless problems. But after Baldur's death, the gods had finally had enough of him. They decided to punish him. First Loki was dragged to a cave. There he was chained to a rock below a huge, poisonous snake. Venom dripped from the snake's mouth onto Loki's face, causing him unbearable pain. His wife, Siguna, tried to catch the venom in a bowl, but the bowl was too small. Every time she emptied it, the poison would drop on Loki again.

Finally Loki would free himself by breaking his chains at the onset of Ragnorok, the vast battle between the giants and the Aesir that would end the universe.

Loki's children took after him and plagued the gods. His children were Fenris, a frightening wolf; Midgard, a hissing serpent; and Hela, the Goddess of Death.

NIORD
God of the Ocean

Niord was one of the Vanir, a second group of Norse gods and goddesses. To keep the peace between the Aesir and the Vanir, the gods agreed to exchange hostages. Odin gave his slow-witted brother, Hoenir, to the Vanir. Niord and his children, Frey and Freya, moved to Asgard.

The ancient Norse were a seafaring people. They built sturdy sailing ships that took them from their seacoast homes to terrorize and colonize distant shores. Fishing and fighting at sea were central to their existence. They needed a god of the ocean, and Niord was that god.

Niord, who lived in a shipyard at the edge of the sea, was not only Ruler of the Oceans, but also God of Wind, Navigation, and Wealth. He created the good winds that sent ships on their way. He taught Norse sailors how to find the right lanes at sea, and he guided them on their voyages. The Norse thanked Niord for making them both prosperous and powerful.

Niord's children were Frey, God of Rain and Sunshine, and Freya, Goddess of Love and Beauty.

FREYA and FREY
Goddess of Love   God of Rain
and Beauty   and Sunshine

The beautiful Freya and her brother, Frey, were the children of Niord.

Freya was Goddess of Love and Beauty—of romance. But Freya had another important duty, one she shared with Odin's warrior-maidens, the Valkyries. With Odin she would ride her cat-drawn chariot to battlefields and gather up half of the fallen warriors. Then she would bring them back to Valhalla, the Hall of the Dead. The Valkyrie would take the other half.

When Freya's husband, Od, left and never returned, she cried herself to sleep with tears of gold.

As God of Rain and Sunshine, Frey was the only god who could assure the growth of crops. He rode a boar with bristles of gold and owned a magic gold sword that slew his enemies by itself.

One day, Frey noticed a beautiful maiden named Gerda. Gerda was the daughter of Angerboda, a giantess who was ugly on one side and beautiful on the other. Frey wanted to marry Gerda, but he had to give up his magic sword in payment. Frey gave up his sword willingly, and Gerda and he were married nine days later.

BRAGI and IDUNN

God
of Poetry

Goddess
of Youth

The youthful Bragi, whose young face was covered by a snow-white beard, was the only one of Odin's sons given the gift of poetry.

Odin had become the first poet when he drank the magic potion he had stolen from Gunnlod, a giantess. But his conscience bothered him. When he learned that he was the father of Gunnlod's son, Bragi, he decided to make amends. He had Bragi sip the magic potion and become the God of Poetry.

Bragi's wife, Idunn, was the Keeper of the Golden Apples of Youth. A single bite from one of her apples kept a god or goddess from growing old.

Once Loki helped a giant kidnap Idunn and her apples. All the Aesir began to age. The gods threatened Loki with terrible pain unless he revealed where Idunn had been taken. Since Loki himself was growing older too, he agreed. He returned to Jotunheim, the land of the giants, and rescued Idunn. Idunn's return brought youth back to Asgard.

Tyr was a warrior, an expert with swords and spears. To the Aesir, Tyr was the bravest warrior-god of all. Yet Tyr's greatest act of courage did not come in battle.

After Odin banished two of Loki's children from Asgard—throwing the serpent Midgard into the sea and sending Hela to her icy palace in Hel—he had to deal with the wolf, Fenris. At first, the other gods wanted to keep Fenris in Asgard. He seemed to be a cuddly, playful puppy. But Fenris grew to become gigantic, with teeth and temper to match. Only Tyr had the courage to bring him his food. The Aesir became so afraid of the wolf that they had him tightly bound. Fenris broke his bonds and became even more menacing. Each time he was tied, he broke free.

The Aesir decide to use chains that could not be broken. They tricked the great wolf into allowing himself to be chained. Fenris agreed to be chained only if Tyr put his right hand between the wolf's jaws. As courageous as always, Tyr placed his hand in the wolf's mouth and the chains were fastened. Fenris could not break free. But in his frantic struggle, he bit off Tyr's hand.

Tuesday, the third day of the week, is named for Tyr.

HEIMDALL
The Watchman

Bifrost, the rainbow bridge between Asgard and Earth, was the most important way into Asgard. Odin's son Heimdall guarded this bridge, because the Aesir worried that the giants would use it to attack them.

Heimdall needed little or no sleep. He could see hundreds of miles in any direction, day or night. He could hear the clouds float by and the grass grow.

Heimdall's post was at the top of the rainbow, where he could watch for giants and other enemies and prevent them from crossing into Asgard. He carried a huge golden trumpet, called Gjallarhorn, to warn the Aesir of any danger. A single blast of the horn would make the stars jump and the earth quiver.

HELA
Goddess of Death

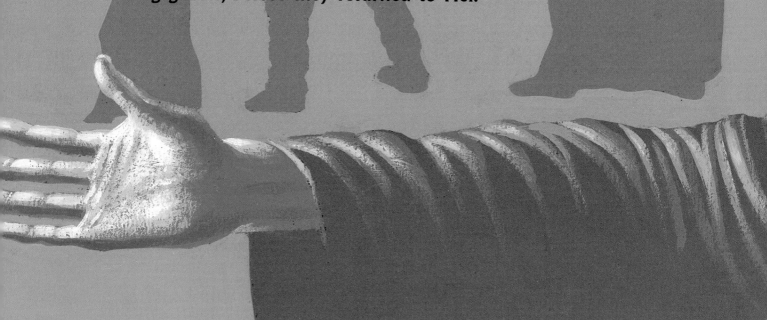

Hela was the daughter of Loki and the giantess Angerboda. She lived in Hel, the realm of the dead, which was forever shrouded in ice and gloom.

In Niffleheim, Odin gave Hela power over the nine regions of Hel. A mile-high fence surrounded a cavernous hall, Elvidner, whose walls were covered with writhing snakes. A howling dog, Garm, guarded the gate. It was there that those who died of old age, sickness, or accidents were greeted by the unsmiling Hela.

Hela, who was pink on one side and blue on the other, would decide where she would send the dead. The most wicked of them were sent to a bleak region, where the monstrous dragon Nidhogg chewed on a root of Yggdrasill, the tree that held up the universe.

Sometimes Hela would forget to close the gates of Hel. Then the dead would wander off to the worlds of the living as shadowy, moaning ghosts, before they returned to Hel.

RAGNAROK
The Last Battle

At some point in the future, the Norse gods and goddesses would have to face their fierce enemies, the giants of Jotunheim. This battle, Ragnarok, would be the final battle between the gods and evil, and it would overwhelm and destroy the universe. All the creatures of Norse myths—the gods, warriors, giants, dwarves, gnomes, and elves—would die in this war.

Even Odin, the King of the Gods, would die, swallowed alive by Loki's son, the terrifying wolf Fenris. But Fenris too would die, killed by Odin's son Vidar.

Mighty Thor would die, choked by the poisonous breath of the serpent Midgard, another of Loki's children. Brave Tyr and the Hound of Hel would kill each other. And finally Heimdall would kill the trickster Loki, though he would perish in the fight.

Once the gods are dead, the last two surviving giants would gulp down the goddesses of Asgard, and then devour the sun, the moon, and the stars. Then they too would disappear. Finally, the great tree Yggdrasill collapses, bringing down the entire universe, leaving behind a cold, empty, and black universe.

After a while, the dark void would give way to a new universe. New worlds would be born. And the gods and goddesses would rise again, to rule a world without evil.

Bibliography

Branston, Brian. *Gods & Heroes from Viking Mythology.* Illustrated by Giovanni Caselli. New York: Schocken Books, 1982.

Bulfinch, Thomas. *Bulfinch's Mythology.* New York: Modern Library, 1998.

Carlyon, Richard, comp. *A Guide to Gods and Goddesses.* New York: Quill, 1981.

D'Aulaire, Ingri and Edgar P. *D'Aulaires' Norse Gods and Giants.* New York: Doubleday and Company, 1967.

Hamilton, Edith. *Mythology.* Boston: Little Brown and Company, 1940.

Harrison, Michael. *The Doom of the Gods.* Oxford: Oxford University Press, 1985.

Pronunciation Guide

Capital letters indicate the stressed syllable.

Aesir: AI-seer

Angerboda: AHNG-er-boh-dah

Baldur: BAHL-der

Bragi: BRAH-gee

Fenris: FEN-riss

Freki (wolf): FREHK-ih

Frey: fry

Freya: FRY-ah

Frigga: FRIG-gah

Garm: gahrm

Gerda: GAIRD-a

Geri (wolf): GE-ree

Gunnlod: GUNE-lawd

Heimdall: HAME-dahl

Hela: HEL-lah

Hermod: HEHR-mood

Holdur: HOL-der

Hoenir: HEH-neer

Hugin (raven): HUE-gin

Idunn: EE-doon

Loki: LOH-kee

Magni: MAHG-nee

Midgard: MID-gahr

Modi: MOH-dee

Munin (raven): MUE-nin

Nanna: NAH-nah

Nidhogg: NEED-hog

Niord: nioor

Od: odd

Odin: OO-den

Sifi: SEE-fee

Siguna: SEE-goon-a

Steipmur (Odin's horse): STEP-moor

Thor: thore

Tyr: teer

Valkyries: vahl-KURE-rees

Vanir: VAH-neer

Vidar: VEE-dahr